AKIMBO
AND THE
CROCODILE MAN

ALEXANDER McCALL SMITH

AKIMBO
and the
CROCODILE MAN

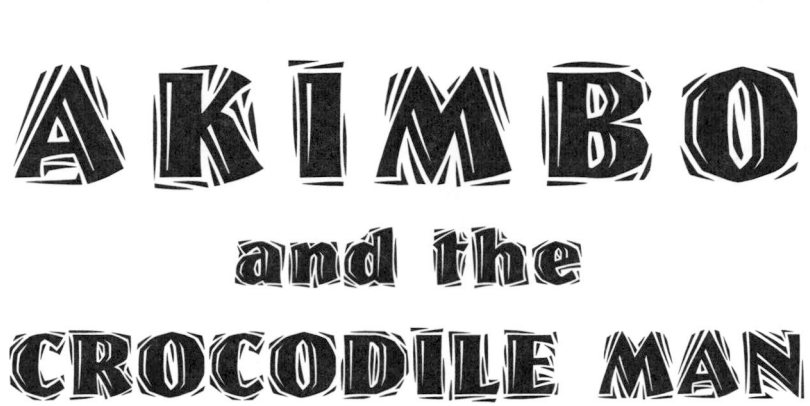

ILLUSTRATED BY LeUyen Pham

BLOOMSBURY
CHILDREN'S
BOOKS

Published by Bloomsbury Publishing, New York, London, and Berlin
Distributed to the trade by Holtzbrinck Publishers

Library of Congress Cataloging-in-Publication Data
McCall Smith, Alexander.
Akimbo and the crocodile man / by Alexander McCall Smith ;
illustrated by LeUyen Pham.—1st U.S. ed.
p. cm.
Summary: Akimbo goes to the rescue of a zoologist who is injured on
his father's game preserve.
ISBN-10: 1-58234-692-5 • ISBN-13: 978-1-58234-692-2
[1.Rescues—Fiction. 2. Crocodiles—Fiction. 3. Game reserves—
Fiction. 4. Africa—Fiction.] I. Pham, LeUyen, ill. II. Title.
PZ7.M47833755Aki 2006   [Fic]—dc22   2005042177

First U.S. Edition 2006

Typeset by Hewer Text UK Ltd, Edinburgh
Printed in Mexico

1 3 5 7 9 10 8 6 4 2

Bloomsbury Publishing, Children's Books, U.S.A.
175 Fifth Avenue, New York, NY 10010

THIS BOOK IS FOR
PHILIP AND MARY MAGEE

CONTENTS

An Unusual Visitor 1

A Dangerous Search Begins 11

Catching a Crocodile! 19

The Baby Crocodiles Arrive 29

Crocodile Attack 35

A Dangerous Swim 45

Getting Help 53

An Unusual Visitor

kimbo was sitting in his favorite cool place on the veranda, looking down the long, dusty road that led to the house. It was the middle of a hot African afternoon, and the bush was alive with the screech of insects. Overhead, the empty blue sky seemed to go on forever and ever. Nothing stirred.

Suddenly Akimbo saw a cloud of dust in the distance. He stood up, straining his eyes to get a better view. Yes, he thought. This is it.

"Look!" he shouted to his mother, who was somewhere inside the house. "Look! Our visitor is coming."

Akimbo's mother joined him on the

veranda. The dust cloud was bigger now, and they could see what was causing it as it bumped its way over the road. It was a large white truck.

"Go and tell your father," she said. "He will want to know that his guest has arrived safely."

Akimbo ran down the path that led to the ranger station. He made his way to the half-open door, with its "Chief Ranger" sign, and peered in.

"Our visitor is here," he said from the doorway.

Akimbo's father looked up from his desk and smiled. He was clearly pleased to hear the news.

"Good," he said. "So the crocodile man has arrived at last!"

When they got back to the house, the white truck had already drawn up at the front door. Akimbo and his father climbed the steps to the veranda, where they found the visitor sitting in one of the canvas chairs, sipping a cup of tea that Akimbo's mother had prepared for him after his long journey.

Akimbo's father shook hands with the man, who then turned to Akimbo and gave him a friendly smile.

"So you're Akimbo," he said. "I've heard a lot about you."

Akimbo reached out shyly and shook the visitor's hand.

"My name's John," said the man.

Akimbo looked up at him. John was very tall, he noticed, and had a warm, friendly face. But there was something else he noticed—all the way down his right arm there ran a long, thick scar, punctured here and there by ridges where welts had healed. Akimbo tried not to stare, but it was hard to avoid doing so, and John noticed the boy's gaze on his arm.

"Yes," he said jokingly. "That was quite a bite."

Akimbo looked away, embarrassed, but it was obvious that John did not mind.

"A crocodile," he said. "Not a big one, actually. It was only a couple of years old, but it took me by surprise and it managed to make quite a mess before I dealt with it."

Akimbo's father gave a shudder. "I've

always kept well away from those creatures,'' he said. ''I don't know what you see in them.''

John laughed. ''But they're fascinating,'' he said. ''They're the most interesting animals in Africa.''

Akimbo's father was not convinced.

''Give me lions anytime,'' he said. ''Or leopards. Or any of the others we have. But crocodiles—no, thank you!''

Akimbo did not see their guest until supper-time that night. His father took John across to the ranger station and the two of them did not return until shortly before seven. As they sat down at the table and began their meal, Akimbo made every effort to keep his eyes off John's injured arm, but once again he found it hard to do so. How had the crocodile gotten him? Had John been in the water or out of it when it happened? And had he saved himself, or had there been somebody there to help him?

As the meal progressed, John turned to Akimbo and began to tell him about himself.

"I'm a zoologist," he said. "I spend all my time studying animals and writing up my findings for people to read."

Akimbo was fascinated. "Have you written a book?" he asked.

John nodded. "Yes," he said. "I've written a book all about crocodiles."

"I've seen it," chipped in Akimbo's father. "They have it in town."

Akimbo was very impressed. He had never met anybody who had written a book before—especially a book about crocodiles. He wondered if he would be able to find it at his school. He doubted it somehow, as there were not many books in the school library, and those that were there seemed to be about science and mathematics and subjects like that. If only there were books about crocodiles!

"And what are you going to be doing here?" asked Akimbo's mother. Like her husband, she did not like crocodiles either.

The crocodile man sat back in his chair.

"I'm going to be starting a project on egg hatching," he said. "I want to try to find out how many of the newly hatched crocodiles survive the first year of life."

Akimbo was surprised to hear about the hatching. He did not even know that crocodiles laid eggs. It seemed strange to think of a great creature like that coming from something as small as an egg. He wondered if you could eat a crocodile's egg, and whether it would taste at all like a hen's egg. He did not want to try this, but perhaps he would find out about it if he managed to get hold of a book on crocodiles.

John went on to explain what he planned to do. He wanted to try to catch a female crocodile and all her baby crocodiles and put tags on them. Then, a year later, he would return to the same spot and see how many of the tagged crocodiles could still be found in the area.

This all sounded really interesting to Akimbo. But how did one tag a crocodile? He could not imagine that it would be easy.

"Won't it be dangerous?" he asked. "I wouldn't like to try to catch the mother crocodile."

John chuckled. "Yes," he replied. "It can be dangerous. In fact, that's how this happened."

He pointed to his torn right arm, answering the question Akimbo had been longing to ask.

"We'll net them," John went on, turning to Akimbo's father. "I'll need three or four of your men," he said. "And perhaps you'd like to help as well?"

Akimbo's father raised his hands in horror. "No, thank you," he said, quickly adding, "but I'm sure that some of my men won't mind helping you."

Akimbo saw his chance. "Nor would I," he blurted out. "I wouldn't mind coming."

There was a silence at the table. The crocodile man turned and looked at Akimbo.

"Are you sure?" he said. "I'd be very happy for you to come and watch."

"I'd love to," said Akimbo as quickly as he could, casting a doubtful glance in his father's direction.

Akimbo's father sighed. They had had this argument before, when Akimbo insisted on going with him to catch a rogue lion that was raiding cattle pens at the edge of the game park. That adventure had ended with Akimbo bringing back a motherless lion cub. Would this one end with a pet crocodile wandering around the place?

"Please," Akimbo begged. "Please say it's all right."

Akimbo's father looked at the crocodile man, then back at his son.

"Very well," he said. "But remember, I don't want you bringing back any little crocodiles."

"I promise I won't," insisted Akimbo.

"And I don't want any part of you bitten off!" added Akimbo's mother sternly. "Not even a little finger!"

"I promise that won't happen either," said John, his eyes sparkling.

And with that it was settled. Akimbo would be a member of the crocodile man's team.

A Dangerous Search Begins

They set off the next morning, just the two of them, Akimbo and his new friend, John. It was a bright, warm morning, and as they traveled over the rough bush road they disturbed a number of animals that were out finding food before the real heat of the day. They saw baboons, several families of warthogs, and, as they turned a corner, a rhinoceros lumbering off into cover.

As they traveled, John talked to Akimbo about crocodiles.

"If you're going to be helping me with my crocodiles," he said, "then you should know something about them."

Akimbo was eager to learn and listened intently as John told him all about the life of the strange reptiles.

"They're just like any other animal," he explained. "Much of their life is spent looking for food and keeping warm."

"So that's why they sunbathe," Akimbo said. He had seen crocodiles resting on sandbanks, soaking up the warmth of the sun like sunbathers on a beach.

John nodded.

"They're cold-blooded," he said. "They have to store up heat from the sun. That's why they lie so still. They don't want to waste any energy."

There were other things too. John told him how the crocodile grabbed its prey, seizing it in its great jaws and then twisting it to tear off the flesh.

"They have terrific power in their jaws," he said, "but it's all directed at snapping the jaws closed. The muscles that open the mouth are much weaker."

Akimbo was fascinated. He had not realized that there was so much to learn about crocodiles, and he could hardly wait to get to the river so that they could start their search.

They stopped some distance short of the river itself.

"I don't want to disturb them," John explained. "We should walk from here, and keep our voices down as well. That way, if there are any crocodiles basking, we should be able to spot them."

They parked the truck under some trees to keep it cool. Then, being as quiet as he could, John led Akimbo through the thick scrub that lay between them and the edge of the river. Akimbo took great care where he put his feet—his father had taught him that this was the secret to moving silently through the bush. There were always twigs or small branches that would crack loudly if you stepped on them.

The river at that point was fairly wide and moved slowly and sluggishly past reed-lined banks. Here and there, the surface of the water was broken by rocks that jutted out like small islands along a coast. There were also sandbanks, spits of golden brown sand that dipped below the green surface of the water. These were ideal places for crocodiles to bask, as they offered all that they needed—warmth, a good view of what was happening on the riverbanks, and an easy way back into the water if danger presented itself.

John crouched down and signaled to Akimbo to do the same. They were still a little way from the edge of the river, but they had good cover, as well as an uninterrupted view of several sandbanks and places where the river widened out into deep, still pools.

"This is an ideal place for them," John whispered. "If we stay here for a while, we're bound to see something."

Akimbo settled down on the ground beside the crocodile man and watched the river in front of him. The water looked so smooth and peaceful that it was difficult to imagine anything as dangerous as a crocodile lurking below it. In fact, as he sat there, he thought how nice and cool it would be to swim! Yet he had only to glance at John's scarred arm to remind himself that swimming was not a good idea.

For a long time nothing seemed to happen. Akimbo began to wonder whether they would ever see anything, but John seemed quite happy to sit patiently, watch the river, and chew at a blade of succulent green river grass that he had plucked.

Akimbo's attention had wandered, and he was looking at a group of chattering birds in a treetop when he felt John tug at his sleeve.

"There!" he said quietly. "On the other side!"

Akimbo looked in the direction John was pointing. On the other side of the river, a few paces away from a sandbank, a dark object was moving slowly across the surface of the water.

"Two of them," John whispered. "The other one's slightly behind."

Akimbo had to search for a while, but at last he picked out the snout of the second crocodile.

A few seconds later, the two crocodiles reached the sandbar and began to lumber up out of the water. As they did so, Akimbo drew in his breath.

"Yes," whispered John. "They're beauties. At least five meters each."

Akimbo had never seen such large crocodiles and could hardly believe that they had been there all along, lurking somewhere in the pools or reeds. He and John watched silently as the two giant reptiles settled themselves on the bank. After a few minutes, the crocodiles became quite immobile, their giant heads resting in the warm sand, their tails stretched out behind them.

"They're not going to be doing very much today," John said, rising to his feet. "I think that we can have a quick look around and then go home."

Akimbo and John both rose to their feet and made their way silently from the bank. John led, picking his way with great caution, avoiding clumps of reed that were too dense to pass through, and taking care not to get too close to the water.

After awhile, the reeds opened up before them and they found themselves on the edge of a broad sandbank. They stopped, making sure that there were no crocodiles on it, and then John went forward, followed by Akimbo.

Akimbo was not sure what John was looking for, but whatever it was, he soon found it.

"Look down there," John said, pointing at the sand before him. "That's what we're after."

Akimbo looked down at the moist sand. There at their feet was a small mound, with some marks in the sand beside it, as if the surface had been scratched by some creature. But there was no other clue as to what it was.

"A crocodile nest," said John, glancing over his shoulder toward the river. "If you've never seen a crocodile's egg, then you're going to see one now!"

CATCHING A CROCODILE!

Gently, like a man uncovering a precious treasure, John brushed away the sand from the top of the nest. The covering was not thick, and soon Akimbo saw the first white of the shells revealed.

John lifted up one of the eggs, cupping it carefully in his hands. He tapped it softly and held it up to the sun. Then he put it to his ear and shook it.

"There's a young crocodile in there," he said. "And it's only a few days from hatching."

Akimbo watched as John put the egg back in place and softly covered the nest with sand again. After a minute or two, the nest was returned to exactly the state in which it had been found, and nobody would have known that it had ever been disturbed.

John stood up and dusted the sand off his hands.

"Good," he said. "I think that's our day's work done. We'll come back here tomorrow, set up our observation post, and watch the young fellows hatch. Then we'll try to tag them, and the mother too. That way we'll be able to keep a record of the whole family."

Akimbo followed John back to the truck, his mind seething with excitement. He wondered if the mother would be one of the massive crocodiles he had seen basking on the sandbank downriver. It would be easy enough to tag the baby crocodiles, he imagined, but to tag the mother would certainly not be a simple task.

They reached home late that night. Akimbo wanted to tell his father all about their day, but he was just too exhausted. The next morning over breakfast, though, he recounted what they had done and took great pleasure in describing the full size of the two basking crocodiles.

"I don't like the sound of that," Akimbo's father said. "Are you sure that you want to carry on with this?"

Akimbo nodded. "And there's a nest too," he said. "We're going to watch the young ones hatch."

John and Akimbo set off later that day. Four men from the ranger station came with them, and in the back of the truck there was heaped what seemed to Akimbo to be a mountain of supplies. There were tents, nets, thick ropes, and several other specialized pieces of equipment that Akimbo did not recognize.

When they reached the river, they had to make several trips by foot, carrying the equipment from the truck to the place near the sandbank where they had located the nest. It was hard work in the heat, but at last everything was piled in one place and could be sorted out.

First, two tents were erected in a place that

gave a view of the sandbank. Then, after John had checked the bank itself, the nets and ropes were carried down to the thick clump of reeds that grew around the edges of the bank. The nets were unwound and put in a position where they could be picked up quickly, and the same was done for the ropes.

After an hour or so, John appeared satisfied with the preparations. He called the men around him and gave each one his instructions. Akimbo was to stay in the tent, he said, when they were using the nets. But at least he could help with the tagging of the little crocodiles.

"Their teeth are pretty small," John said. "They can't give you much more than a nip."

With everything in place, they made their way back to the tents and sat inside them, grateful for the shade. Now there was nothing to do but sit and wait.

It was one of the men who saw the crocodile first. He whispered to John, who looked out and nodded. Akimbo peered out from the mouth of the tent and saw the black shape at the edge of the sandbank, just below the surface of the water. He could tell that it was a crocodile, and a large one at that.

Now John and the men crept out of the tent and soon disappeared into the bank of reeds. Akimbo watched, his heart thumping with excitement, as the crocodile moved up onto the sandbank. She stopped near the nest and seemed to stay quite still, as if she were guarding it. It must be the mother, thought Akimbo. Had she sensed that somebody had disturbed the nest?

For a few minutes nothing happened. Then Akimbo saw the reeds at the far end of the bank move. He saw the heads of two of the men, and he thought he spotted a piece of net. Then, on the other side of the bank, John's head appeared. Akimbo held his breath. Whatever was going to happen would surely happen soon.

There was a sudden shout, and Akimbo saw the crocodile lurch around and make a dash for the water's edge. It would take her no more than a few seconds to be back in her element, but that was enough time for John

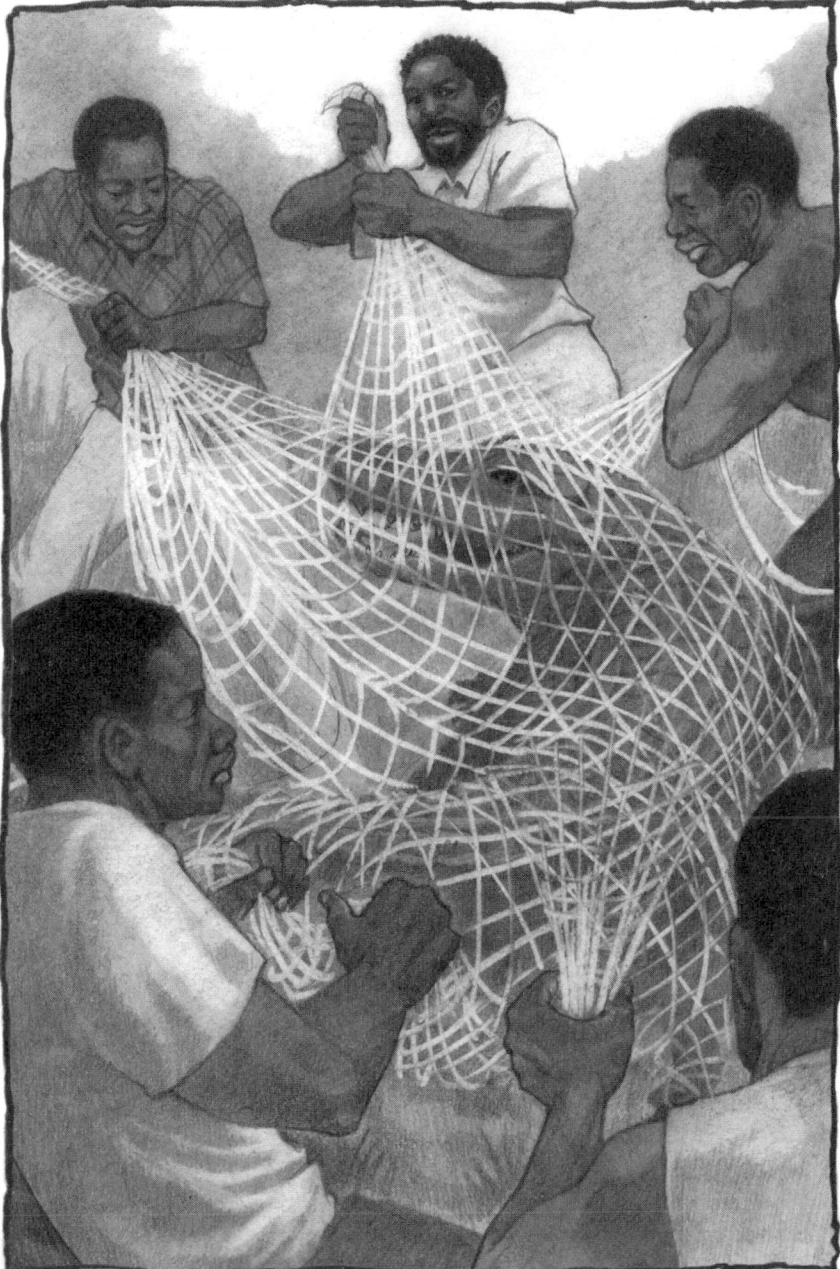

to dart across the sand, dragging one of the nets behind him.

The crocodile continued her plunge, but it was too late, and she lunged headlong into the net. As she did so, two more of the men came out and threw the folds of another net over the struggling beast.

It seemed to Akimbo as if the whole sandbank had erupted into movement. The crocodile turned and thrashed with her tail, but all she did was enmesh herself more firmly in the net. It was impossible for her to escape.

Now John came with a rope and began to loop it around the crocodile's tail. Then more rope was brought, and soon the whole struggling mixture of beast and net was firmly trussed in straining coils of rope.

John looked up and beckoned to Akimbo.

"It's safe now," he called. "She can't do much like this."

Akimbo ran down to the sandbank and stood beside John as they examined their still-writhing, but helpless, captive. A rope had been wound around her jaws so she could not open them. Her tail, too, had been secured, although it still twisted and battled against the restraint.

"We'll waste no time," said John. "We don't want to harm her."

With that, he picked up a curious implement that had been laid to one side. This was the tagging device, and John quickly snipped a metal tag between its jaws. Then, approaching the crocodile carefully, he selected one of the bumps along the top of her tail and clipped the tag into the skin.

"Won't that hurt her?" Akimbo asked.

"She won't feel a thing," John reassured him. "But she's marked from now on."

John left the crocodile's side.

"Now," he said. "Here comes the difficult part. Akimbo, you stand back while we let her free."

It was not simple disentangling an angry crocodile, but at last the final fold of net was dragged away and the reptile found herself free. With a great hissing sound, she shot away, plunging into the river with a splash.

John signaled to the men to leave, and

together they all abandoned the bank and clambered back up to the tent.

"Now we have to wait for the hatching," John explained to Akimbo. "And that's going to be fun."

THE BABY CROCODILES ARRIVE

They had brought enough provisions for four days. John thought that the eggs were due to hatch soon, but he could not be certain.

"There's nothing to do but wait," he said. "They'll hatch sooner or later."

They did not hatch that day, nor that night. At nighttime, every two hours one of the men crept down to the sandbank to see if anything had happened. Each time, the report was the same: the mound of sand was undisturbed.

At first Akimbo tried to keep awake, so that he would not miss any of the excitement, but John assured him that he would rouse him if anything happened. When Akimbo awoke the next morning, with the first rays of the sun streaming in through the mouth of the tent, one of the men was just returning from the sandbank.

"Nothing," he said, shaking his head. "Nothing at all."

The watch continued. At midmorning they drank tea, brewed by one of the men, and at midday they had lunch. Then, as the pots that the men had used to cook the maize meal were being packed away, John gave a low whistle.

"All right, everyone," he said. "Things are beginning to happen."

They made their way down to the sandbank as quickly as they could, but even though they hurried, they missed the first of the newly hatched crocodiles. Part of the sand covering the nest had been scraped away, and the top of a shattered and empty egg was exposed to the sun.

They stood around the nest, watching the miracle that was being performed before their very eyes. The next egg was breaking

now, cracking across the top to reveal a struggling, slimy creature within. Then a snout appeared, the tip of a tail, and within moments a complete and perfect tiny crocodile had scurried out onto the sand.

John reached forward and plucked the midget creature from the ground. Then, expertly closing the tiny, snapping jaws, he applied a small, shining tag to the tail. It took no more than a few seconds, after which the little creature was dropped back on the sand to scurry off toward the water.

The rest followed smoothly. All the eggs were now exposed, and over the next hour or so almost all of them cracked open and hatched a tiny crocodile. Each was tagged and pointed down toward the water. Each disappeared into the river within seconds. Only a few eggs, which John said were infertile, did not open. These were carefully packed away for further examination.

As John performed his work, two of the men kept watch at the end of the sandbank.

"The mother will be around here somewhere," John said. "But she probably won't dare come out. There are too many of us for her."

When all the baby crocodiles had been tagged, John, who had counted each one, made an entry in a book and gathered up his equipment. It was now time to go, to pack up the tent and leave the crocodiles in peace—at least for the time being.

"We can come back tomorrow," John said to Akimbo. "If we look very carefully, we might be able to spot these youngsters around the edge of the river. Would you like that?"

Akimbo said that he would. It had been a most extraordinary sight seeing the tiny crocodiles emerging into the world, and he hoped with all his heart that they would be alive the next day. John had explained to him that there were all sorts of dangers facing crocodiles in their first few days. They could even be eaten by large birds, he said; a heron could pick up and swallow a newly hatched crocodile just as it would swallow a fish.

"Their mother will be able to protect them some of the time," he went on. "Do you know that she shelters her young inside her jaws for the first few days?''

Akimbo found it hard to imagine. If he were looking for shelter, he thought that the inside of a crocodile's mouth would be the very last place he would try!

CROCODILE ATTACK

They returned to the river the next day without any of the men from the ranger station. It would be better for them to go alone, said John, as the presence of more people just meant more disturbance and less chance of seeing crocodiles. Besides, John planned to launch his inflatable boat on the river, and it had room for only two.

Akimbo was excited at the prospect of going in the boat, and he was even more thrilled when John said he could start off rowing it.

"Take it gently," said John. "We're in no hurry, and the last thing we want to do is end up in the water!"

They eased the small boat into the river and then, while John held the bow, Akimbo waded out as deep as his knees and climbed aboard. John followed him and then pushed away from the shore with the metal oar. Soon the gentle current of the river had picked them up and begun to carry them downstream.

Akimbo found rowing harder than he had imagined, but he soon mastered it and had them moving slowly upriver against the current. They stayed out in the middle, well away from any rocks or shallows, and watched the reed banks move slowly past.

By the time they were nearing the sandbank where the hatching had taken place, Akimbo's arms were tired of rowing and he willingly handed the oars over to John.

John dipped the blades into the water so gently that there was hardly a ripple. He was watching the edge of the water intently now, and suddenly he gestured sharply to Akimbo.

"That's them," he whispered, pointing toward a reedy part of the bank.

Akimbo stared at the water's edge but

could see nothing. Then he noticed a little movement, and then another. In the meantime, John had turned the boat and was slowly approaching the edge. As the boat drifted into the reeds, he handed the paddle to Akimbo and then, without warning, his hand darted out and plucked a glistening little crocodile from the water.

He held the little creature out toward Akimbo and pointed to its tail. There was the tag, still in position, identifying it as one of theirs.

"He's made it to his second day," John said, laughing as he dropped the tiny crocodile back into the water. "Good luck!"

They found three more shortly after that, and then John took the paddle again and propelled the boat out into the middle of the river. They made their way farther upstream, traveling quietly, as John hoped to see other crocodiles on sandbanks farther up. But the riverbank seemed deserted for the time being, although Akimbo knew well that this did not mean there were no crocodiles about.

*   *   *

They had negotiated several bends in the river when they came across the island. It was at a point where the river broadened out considerably and was fairly shallow in parts. The island was not big, but it supported a fair amount of vegetation, including a clump of tall, heavy-leaved trees. John was delighted to have found it and quickly paddled the boat over to a muddy beach about halfway along one side.

They beached the boat and got out to explore. John wanted to see if there were any sandy places that might be used by crocodiles for hatching. Akimbo wanted to walk from one end to the other, just to see what it was like.

"Be careful of snakes," John warned as Akimbo made his way up to the ridge that ran through the middle of the island. "Have a look around, and then come back here."

Akimbo climbed up to the top of the ridge and looked down. John had left the boat on the muddy beach and was making his way through the reeds, looking for signs of crocodiles.

Akimbo turned away and began his exploration of the island. There was not much to see, though. There were no animals, although he thought he saw monkeys in a tree at one point, and there were no interesting rocks or caves. All in all, he thought as he reached the tip of the island and turned back, it's a boring place.

It was then that he heard the cry. It was a shout, a yell, and it came from the other end of the island. Akimbo stopped in his tracks and listened, but all he heard was the screeching of cicadas and the sound of calling birds. Then there was another cry, and this time Akimbo knew.

Running wildly, blindly, his heart pumping fear into his limbs, Akimbo crashed through the undergrowth. It took him only a few minutes until he was at the point of the ridge from which he had set out. And there, below him, he saw John, half in the water and half out, struggling and calling out in a mass of foaming water.

Akimbo half-jumped, half-fell down the ridge, and reached out to grab his friend.

He knew what was happening, but he had little idea how to help.

"The paddle!" shouted John. "Get the paddle!"

Akimbo spun around and reached for the paddle that lay beside the boat. In an instant, he noticed that the boat had been ripped and was now a deflated piece of limp rubber.

Akimbo seized the paddle, raised it in the air, and brought it down with all his strength on the twisting dark shape that seemed to have attached itself to John's leg. There was a dull thud and the shock of contact. Akimbo raised the paddle once more and brought it down again with all his force.

At the second blow, the dark shape seemed to lurch backward and then, in a froth of foam and churning water, was gone. The river calmed, and Akimbo saw John stagger out of the shallows where he had been struggling with his attacker. Safely back on the mud bank, he slumped backward and pulled himself the last few inches out of the water.

Akimbo knelt beside his friend. He looked

at his leg and saw that it had been bitten terribly. Bright red blood streaked down, staining the mud beside the injured limb. Without hesitation, Akimbo slipped off his shirt and bound it quickly around the wound, making it as tight as he could in an effort to stanch the flow of blood.

"Thank you," said John, his voice thick and shaky. "You came just in time."

The bandage seemed to be having its effect and the flow of blood slowed down to a trickle. John tried to stand, but the injured leg would not support him, and he fell back against the mud.

"It's no use," he said. "I think a bone's broken."

Akimbo glanced at the boat, and John shook his head sadly.

"He attacked me just as I was trying to launch it," he said. "I was going to come around to the other end to pick you up there. He got me as I pulled it out."

Akimbo looked at John's wounded leg again. He would have to get help soon, as the bleeding had not stopped altogether and there was a limit to the amount of blood that could be lost. And yet, with the boat destroyed, there seemed to be no way of getting that help. Could they just wait it out? How long would it be before a search party found them? It could be a day or two, or even more. And if it took that long, would John survive the terrible injury the crocodile had inflicted on him?

Akimbo thought not. He would have to go for help himself. There was no other way.

A Dangerous Swim

'll swim across," said Akimbo. "Then I'll go downriver until I get to the truck. I'm sure I can drive it."

John shook his head. "You can't go into that water," he said firmly. "You wouldn't make it. There are too many crocodiles around here."

"I could swim quickly," said Akimbo. "I'm a strong swimmer."

John raised his voice, half in pain, half to show Akimbo that he meant it when he told him not to do it. "No," he said. "You can't. You wouldn't make it."

Akimbo looked out at the river. Perhaps there was a place where it was shallow enough to wade across; perhaps there was a place with stones. But the river, although not always deep, was not that shallow. The only way of crossing was to swim, or . . . Akimbo smiled. Yes. He remembered the fallen branch he had seen just a little way up the ridge. He had had to step over it, and he thought how it could have made a good canoe.

He turned to John and explained his plan enthusiastically. He could roll the branch down to the bank and launch it from there. It might not be the perfect boat, but at least it would float. The paddle had survived the encounter with the crocodile, and he could use that to propel the log across to the other side.

John seemed doubtful. "You're still going to have your legs in the water," he said. "And the log might not be so easy to steer. You could find yourself floating downstream for hours."

"It's not that big," argued Akimbo. "I'm sure I'll manage."

He looked at John's injured leg. Blood was still seeping through the bandage.

"I've got to get help," Akimbo said. "There's no other way."

John gave a wince of pain. He knew that Akimbo was right, and so at last he nodded his reluctant agreement to the plan.

Akimbo did not waste time. Scampering up to the top of the ridge, he found the fallen branch and roughly manhandled it down to the bank. It was hard work, and the bark of the branch was rough on his hands, but eventually he managed to move it into position and the log was floating, half-submerged, at the edge of the river.

Akimbo made sure that John was as comfortable as possible. Then, picking up the paddle, he waded out gingerly and clambered onto his improvised boat.

John had been right about paddling a log. It was much more difficult than Akimbo had imagined, and for the first few minutes Akimbo's efforts seemed to make no impression on the floating branch. Then, slowly, it began to respond, and the boy and his unusual boat began to edge out into the broad stream of the river.

To begin with, Akimbo did not have enough time to think about the danger he was in. All his attention was focused on remaining upright, as the branch seemed to want to roll with the current. If I fall in, he thought, that's the end.

He tried not to think of the giant crocodiles they had seen on the sandbank a few days before. He tried particularly hard not to think of what might be below him in the water at that very moment. But it was impossible not to be afraid, and Akimbo was more frightened than he had ever been in his life.

After a few minutes the log was in midstream. There was a stronger current now, and Akimbo felt the log begin to turn its bow downriver. He paddled harder, in an attempt to direct it toward the bank, but this only made it dip and buck against him. He stopped paddling for a moment and the movement stopped.

Then, without warning, the log twisted strongly to one side. It might have been something that Akimbo did, or it might have struck a submerged obstacle, but the movement took Akimbo by surprise and he felt his balance going. He pulled the paddle over to the other side in a frantic attempt to stay upright, but it was too late, and he felt himself toppling.

Akimbo entered the water with a splash, feeling its treacherous embrace all around him. Relieved of his weight, the log reared up in the water and moved off swiftly with the current.

Akimbo struggled up to the surface. He had lost the log, he had lost the paddle, and in a terrible moment of understanding he felt himself completely alone in the crocodile-infested water.

Instinctively he struck out for the shore, battling desperately to quell the panic within him. He tried to swim as quietly as possible, moving his hands through the water without splashing. He knew that any unusual sound or movement could attract crocodiles, and so his best chance was to move through the water as smoothly as he could.

Something brushed against Akimbo's leg, and for an instant he froze, sinking in terror.

But nothing else happened. What he touched could have been anything—a fish, a piece of weed, a sunken branch. He started to swim again, although the river's edge seemed as far away as ever.

Suddenly Akimbo felt ground beneath his feet. It was soft, slippery mud, but it made his heart soar. He lunged forward, half-swimming, half-walking, and was soon out of the water, hardly believing that he had made it to safety.

For a few minutes he sat on the bank and rested, recovering his strength. Then, rising to his feet, he began the journey back to the place where the truck had been parked.

Getting Help

kimbo started on his journey, running as fast as he could through the thick bush. Sharp branches whipped at him as he ran past, thorns tore at his skin, but he felt nothing. His heart pumping wildly within him, he pushed himself to go faster, ignoring the stitch that had begun to needle at his side. But at last he could run no more, and he slowed down and rested. Looking back, it seemed to him as if he had traveled hardly any distance at all.

"It's easy in a boat," he said to himself. "It takes five times longer on foot."

He stood for a few minutes, gulping in the

air, waiting to get his breath back. Then, his heart beating less wildly, he began to trot off again, keeping the bank of the river just within sight but avoiding the thick reed beds that lined the water's edge. His feet were sore, as one of his shoes had lost part of its sole and was pinching him at each step. He tried to put most of his weight on his other leg, but this just slowed him down even more. So, bending down to undo his laces, he pulled off both shoes and went ahead barefoot.

For almost an hour, Akimbo fought his way through the heavy bush until at last, just when he was beginning to think that he might never reach it, he saw in the distance the clump of trees where the truck was parked. He put on an extra spurt of speed now, leaping over the narrow, overgrown ditches that cut across the land, paying no attention to the sharp stones that dug into the soles of his feet.

"I'll make it after all," he muttered to himself. "I'll save you, John!"

The truck was half in the shade, half in the

sun, and as a result it had become boiling hot. As Akimbo opened the door of the cab, a solid wall of heat came out to greet him. He slid into the cab and pulled the door closed behind him. Then he reached forward to start the engine.

It was at this point that he made an awful discovery. There was no key. For a moment, his mind went blank. Why had he not thought about it? How could he have been so stupid? The key, of course, was probably in John's pocket—why had he not thought to ask him for it? John had no doubt realized this already. Perhaps he had called out to him after he left, to remind him, and he had not heard.

Akimbo leaned forward, his eyes filling with tears. He would never rescue John now. If he ran all the way back to get the key—which would take him much longer now that he was tired—he would have to come all the way back again. And then it would probably be too late to save John, and it would all be his fault for forgetting something as simple as the key of the truck.

Just as he was thinking this, an image came into Akimbo's mind. It was his father talking to him, telling him what he had told him once before when they had both been faced with a problem that seemed insoluble.

"Never give up," his father had said. "Think of other ways of doing what you have to do. You'll be surprised at how often that works!"

Akimbo could almost hear his father's voice. *Think of other ways of doing what you have to do.* Yes! There was another way, but would he be able to do it? Akimbo was very uncertain, but at least he could try.

Akimbo remembered that he had once seen one of his father's assistants start a truck without the key. He had watched carefully, as it interested him, and he thought at the time that it was really rather easy. The man had taken a short length of wire and connected two points behind the ignition. Then, after he had bridged two other points, the engine had swung into life, as if by magic. He had explained it carefully to Akimbo, and he had pointed out just where the wires must touch. But would Akimbo remember it?

It was not difficult to find two short pieces of wire in the tool box that the truck carried. Then, getting down on his hands and knees, Akimbo peered under the dashboard. It was a maze of wires, but he was soon able to see just where the key slotted into the ignition and to make out the points that had to be bridged.

Gingerly, willing his hands not to shake, Akimbo moved the two ends of one of the pieces of wire into position. There was a clicking sound, and he noticed a bulb behind the instrument panel grow red. That was the first step, and he had done it correctly. Now he reached for the other pieces of wire and very carefully bridged the point between the two ends of what he thought must be the starter switch.

As the wire touched the contacts, Akimbo let out a scream. A powerful current of electricity shot into his fingers and his hand and snaked its way up his arm. As it did so, the engine leapt to life and, to Akimbo's horror, the truck lurched forward. In his eagerness to get the truck started, Akimbo had forgotten to check that the gears were disengaged. Now he had started the truck, just as he wanted to, but he was on the floor, and the steering wheel was spinning as the truck began to career off.

Akimbo struggled to pull himself up. The movement of the truck did not help, but at last he managed to wrench himself up onto the seat and grab the steering wheel. The truck had built up some speed in the short time that it had been running, and Akimbo saw, looming before them, the shape of a large tree. He was sure that it was too late, that he would collide with the tree, and he inadvertently closed his eyes as he pulled at the wheel and tried to bring the charging truck away from its course.

There was no sickening thud. There was no sound of crumpling metal. Akimbo opened his eyes and saw that he had just missed the large tree and was bumping

harmlessly over an open patch of grass. Now he pushed in the clutch, changed to a lower gear, and felt the large machine respond to his control. Slowly he swung the wheel around, bringing the truck into the direction he wanted it to follow. It did just as he asked it, and for the first time since the disappointment of finding that he had no key, Akimbo began to feel optimistic about his chances of saving John.

At last Akimbo found his way back onto one of the major roads that led to the ranger camp. He set off, driving as fast as he dared, hoping that when he arrived at the camp his father would be there. He imagined John lying on the island, his leg throbbing with pain. He imagined the crocodiles, watching from the shadows, waiting for their victim to weaken to the point where he would be easy prey. There was no time to lose.

He had been driving for only ten minutes or so when he saw one of the other ranger trucks coming toward him quickly. It seemed almost too good to be true! Akimbo pulled over, disengaged the gears, and applied the brake. Then, as the other truck drew level with him and stopped, its surprised driver leaned out of his window and called out.

"Akimbo! What on earth are you up to?"

Akimbo explained as quickly as he could. Then, leaving his truck by the side of the road, he leapt into the other vehicle, and the driver did everything he could to get them to the riverbank in less than half an hour. Fortunately, he had been making his way to another part of the river, and there was another inflatable boat in the back of the truck. This they launched in record time, and they found John half-sitting, half-lying at the top of the island bank, his injured leg straight out before him.

Akimbo could tell that John was in pain, but in spite of this he still seemed cheerful.

"That was quick," said John. "I was all set for a much longer wait."

"I was worried that the crocodiles would get you," Akimbo said. "Did you see them?"

"No," said John. "But they were there all right. I think that they were, well, I think that they were *interested*!"

They soon had John in the boat and they made the short crossing to the other side. Then Akimbo helped to carry the injured man to the truck, where he was laid out on some empty sacks. After that, there was the rapid drive to the hospital, which was almost fifty miles away. John bumped around a lot in the back of the truck, but he did not complain. He even managed to smile as Akimbo told him all about the way he had started the truck without the key.

"I didn't even think of it," said John. "It's just as well you're a mechanic!"

They watched John being wheeled into the small bush hospital.

"There's no point in waiting," said the ranger who had driven them there. "They'll let us know how things go. I'm sure that everything will be all right!"

And he was right. The next day Akimbo

received a telephone call from the doctor to announce that all was well.

"The bandage stopped the bleeding," the doctor said. "Without it, I don't think he would have made it."

Three days later, Akimbo's father took him to the small bush hospital to visit John. He found him in a little room, propped up against several thick pillows, writing in a notebook.

"So!" said John, laying aside the book. "My rescuer!"

Akimbo smiled modestly. "It wasn't hard," he said. "The only time I was afraid was when I fell in."

John nodded. "I'm glad I didn't see that," he said. "That place was itching with crocs."

"Perhaps they weren't hungry," said Akimbo.

"Or perhaps they didn't like the taste of me," joked John. "That might have put them off for a while."

They talked for a time, until John asked Akimbo to fetch a parcel that was sitting on the table on the other side of the room.

"Open it," he said. "It's for you. It's a little present for what you did."

Akimbo unwrapped the parcel and found himself holding a large book. There, on the cover, was a picture of a crocodile on a bank, and there was John's name in large, black print. It was John's book on crocodiles, the one Akimbo had so wanted to read.

Akimbo opened the book. On the first page, written boldly in ink, was the inscription: "For Akimbo. Thank you." And beneath it was John's signature.

"You may have had enough of crocodiles for the time being," said John. "But maybe you'll read it someday."

"I'll start right away," said Akimbo.

John mused for a moment. "Next year," he said, "when I come back to check up on that family in the river, will you give me a hand?"

"Of course," said Akimbo. "I'll be there."

John looked pleased.

"I think we'll make a crocodile man out of you one of these days," he said, laughing as he spoke.

"I'd like that," said Akimbo. "I really would."

GRAHAM CLARK

A Note on the Author

ALEXANDER McCALL SMITH has written more than fifty books, including the *New York Times* bestselling *No. 1 Ladies' Detective Agency* mysteries and *The Sunday Philosophy Club*. A professor of medical law at Edinburgh University, he was born in what is now Zimbabwe and taught law at the University of Botswana. He lives in Edinburgh, Scotland. Visit him at www.alexandermccallsmith.com.

MARK MULGREW

A Note on the Illustrator

LEUYEN PHAM is the illustrator of numerous award-winning books for children including *Big Sister, Little Sister* (which she also wrote); *Sing-Along Song*; and *Piggies in a Polka*. She lives in San Francisco, California. Visit her at www.leuyenpham.com.

AFRICAN WILDLIFE FOUNDATION®

You can learn all about elephants and lions and cheetahs and zebras and giraffes and other wildlife by visiting the African Wildlife Foundation at www.awf.org.

After you learn about the wild animals, you can help save them—by supporting the African Wildlife Foundation.

The African Wildlife Foundation has worked with the people of Africa for forty-five years. They train park rangers, like Akimbo's father, to protect wildlife and catch poachers. They give scholarships to girls and boys like Akimbo so they can grow up and learn to be scientists who protect Africa's mighty rivers and great forests.